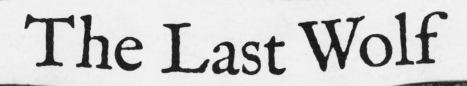

The Last Wolf

Mini Grey

JONATHAN CAPE
LONDON

To Scarlet

JONATHAN CAPE

UK | USA | Canada | Ireland | Australia
India | New Zealand | South Africa

Jonathan Cape is part of the Penguin Random House group of companies
whose addresses can be found at global.penguinrandomhouse.com.

www.penguin.co.uk   www.puffin.co.uk   www.ladybird.co.uk

 Penguin
Random House
UK

First published 2018

001

Copyright © Mini Grey, 2018

The moral right of the author/illustrator has been asserted
Printed in China

A CIP catalogue record for this book is available from the British Library

ISBN: 978-0-857-55092-7

All correspondence to:
Jonathan Cape, Penguin Random House Children's
80 Strand, London WC2R 0RL

One day Little Red put on her hunting hat and boots, flung her popgun on her back, packed up her lunch box with some supplies, and said to her Mum:

"I'm off to catch a wolf."

That's all right, thought Red's Mum to herself.

There hasn't been a wolf around here for at least a hundred years.

"Good luck, Red," she said, "and don't be late for tea."

Red went a-stalking through the forest.

She lurked
behind a tree,
and jumped
out on . . .

a bin bag.

She slithered through the bracken,
and pounced on . . .

a tree stump.

Red wandered
deeper into
the forest.

Red started to run.

She ran and tripped –

It grew shadowy and she lost her path. There were whooling noises and grabby twigs.

but what was this?

Some sort of door?

She tried the doorknob
and knocked and banged . . .

and the door
was opened by . . .

the Last Wolf
in the land.

The Last Wolf was living in a cosy tree-cave,

along with the Last Lynx and the Last Bear.

"You must be a human child,"
said the Last Wolf.
"I've never seen one up close before.
Come in and sit down –
you're just in time for some tea."

"I didn't
know wolves
drank tea,"
said Red.

"There may be
quite a few things
you don't know,"
said the Last Wolf.

They gave Red
a cup of tea
and
told her
about

the
GOOD OLD
DAYS...

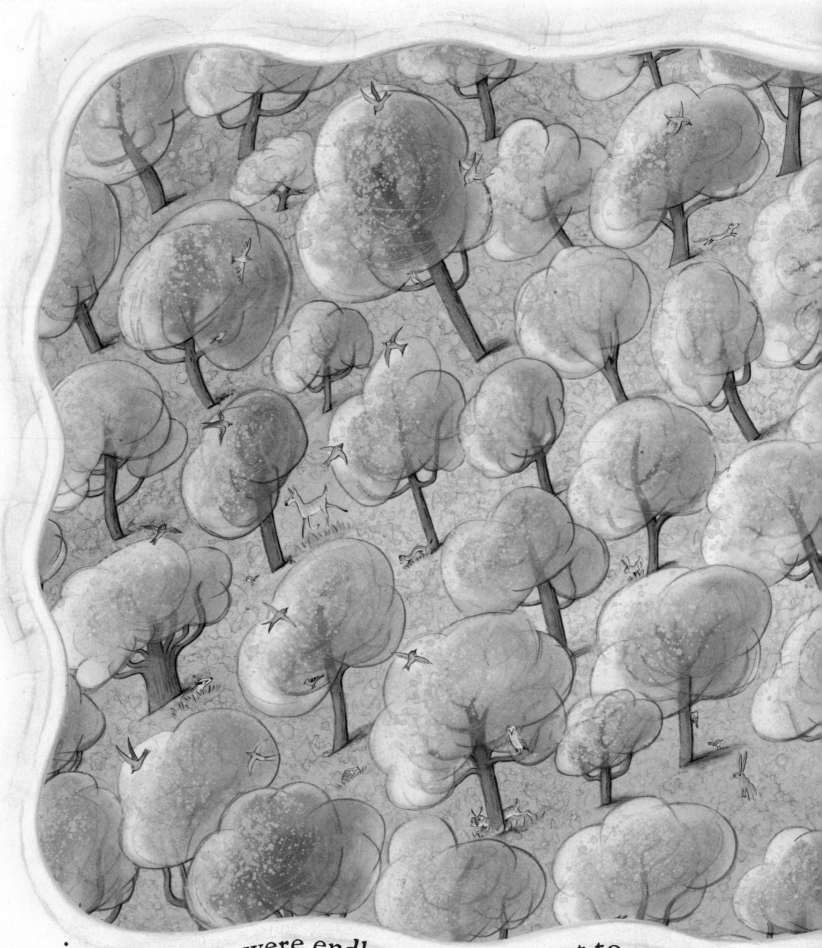

... when there were endless miles of forest to run through

and a thousand tasty grazing beasts to bite . . .

. . . when the world was awash
with flowers and bees
and dripping with honey . . .

... when you could just
lie on a branch

and wait for lunch
to wander right
under your paws.

Nowadays catching a square meal is a difficult business.

The pickings are slim, and the packaging is hard to get into.

They looked longingly
at Little Red.
"My, what huge hungry eyes
you all have," she said . . .

. . . and out of her lunch box she took:

a hard-boiled egg,

a sausage roll,

a chicken sandwich

and an apple.

"It's not very fast on its feet, this Egg," said the Wolf.

"It's quite easy to catch, this Sausage Roll," said the Bear.

The Last Lynx chased
the chicken sandwich
round and round
the cave
until it was
wounded.

Red ate
the apple
and wondered
how she could help.

But it had grown late.

"It's getting dark," said Red, "and I need to go. My Mum will be starting to miss me."

She thought of the Shadowy Wild Wood that was waiting outside.

"I think," said the Last Wolf, "we'd better walk with you till you find your path."

So Little Red,

and the Last Wolf, and the Last Bear,

and the Last Lynx

wound their way back

through the Last Woods that were left . . .

...until they reached the very Last Tree, and saw the lights of Red's home...

...and her Mum missing her.

"Don't forget your lunch box," said the Last Bear.

"Goodbye,
you wild things,"
said Red.
"I think I know
what you need."

But they had
already gone.

After dinner, Red's Mum found a sign on Red's bedroom door.

WaNtED
MoRe
TReeS
pLeaSE
If you see
Some-TeLL RED

"Well, we'd better make some," said Red's Mum.

"All you need is a seed, some earth, sun, air, water and . . .

. . . for a really wonderful tree, about a hundred years."

One day these trees
will be
amazing.

ALL wild THings wELcOME